THE 39 STEPS

Adapted by Russell Punter

Illustrated by Matteo Pincelli

Reading consultant: Alison Kelly
Roehampton University

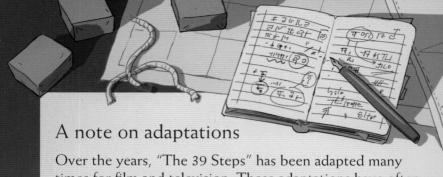

A note on adaptations

Over the years, "The 39 Steps" has been adapted many times for film and television. These adaptations have often included elements that differ from the original book.

For example:

The 39 Steps
-is an organization of spies that has persuaded Mr. Memory, a music hall entertainer, to memorize vital British military secrets (1935 and 1959 films).
-is the number of steps in a section of the bell tower of Big Ben (1978 film).

The character of Scudder
-is a female spy, named Anabella Smith (1935 film) and Miss Robinson (1959 film).

The leader of the spies
-is a seemingly respectable professor, who is missing the top joint from one finger (1935 and 1959 films).
-is a traitor in the British Government (1978 film).

In addition, scenes of Hannay jumping from a train on the Forth Rail Bridge, becoming handcuffed to a beautiful woman, and dangling from the hands of Big Ben's clock face, occur only in the film versions of the story.

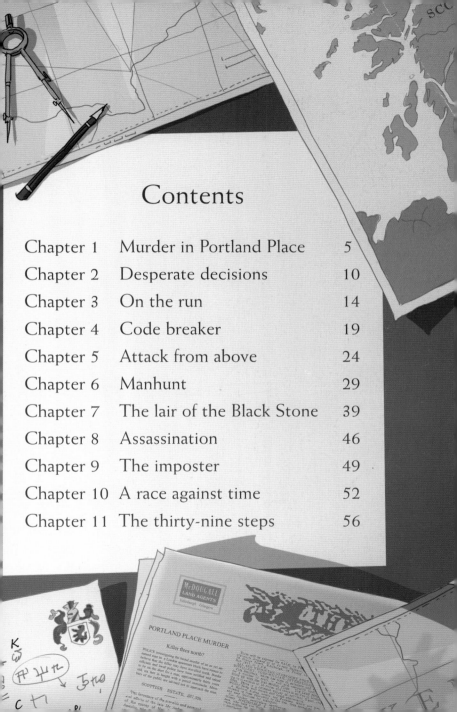

Contents

Chapter 1

Murder in Portland Place

On that muggy June night in 1914, I must admit that I was feeling rather fed up with London.

Having spent most of my life as a mining engineer in the wilds of Rhodesia, my return to England had been tediously dull by comparison.

Yet as I approached my rented house that evening, little could I have imagined the breathtaking adventures that lay ahead of me.

I had just turned my key in the lock, when a slim, bearded man appeared from nowhere and bundled me indoors.

"What the devil...?" I began.

"Pardon the intrusion, Mr. Hannay," panted the stranger.

He dashed across to the window and peered down cautiously at the street below.

"How do you know my name?" I asked.

"Oh, I know a fair deal about you," he replied, drawing the curtains. "Chiefly that you're a man to be trusted."

Despite my better judgement, I was intrigued by the young fellow.

"My name is Scudder, Franklin P. Scudder," he announced. "And I need your help, sir."

"I'll listen to you," I replied, switching on the light. "But that's all I'll promise."

Scudder took a seat with his back to the window. "Mr. Hannay, here in London, on June fifteenth, an attempt will be made to assassinate a man named Karolides."

I'd read about this Karolides in the papers. He was the Greek Premier and just about the only one who could prevent a war in Europe, by all accounts.

"If I can lie low 'til that date," continued Scudder, "I might prevent a catastrophe."

"But who would want Karolides dead?" I asked.

"A group of foreign agents known as the Black Stone. They're on my tail, and they'll stop at nothing to get me." The young man's eyes darted towards the window. "The head of that illustrious organization is particularly interested in making my acquaintance."

The look on his face spoke volumes. This gang leader was obviously a force to be reckoned with.

"He's a master of disguise, Mr. Hannay," he went on, raising his right hand, "but if ever you encounter a man missing the top joint of his fourth finger, then be on your guard."

The whole tale seemed far-fetched. Yet if this fellow was spinning me a yarn, he was a darn good actor.

I thought for a moment. I'd wanted excitement. Well here it was, right on my own doorstep.

"Very well, I'll trust you," I said at last. "I believe you're straight — but if not, I should warn you that I'm a handy man with a gun."

He clasped my hand in his. "Thank you, Mr. Hannay," he said warmly. "You won't know I'm here."

The next four days passed rapidly and Scudder was as good as his word. He spent most of his time closeted in my study, scribbling away in a small black notebook.

Then, on the fifth day, I returned home in the early hours of the morning.

I switched on the hall light and opened the drawing room door. The scene illuminated before me sent a shudder of horror down my spine.

There upon the floor lay the body of Franklin P. Scudder – pierced through the heart by a knife.

Chapter 2

Desperate decisions

Having assured myself that poor Scudder's killers were no longer in residence, I considered my position. The devils must be aware that Scudder would have taken me into his confidence. How long before they tried to dispose of me in a similar fashion?

And here I was with a dead body in my home. If I went to the police, they were hardly likely to believe my story about assassination attempts and foreign agents. What I needed was evidence... Of course, the notebook!

My earlier inspection of the house had alerted me to the fact that Scudder's killers had been looking for something. Drawers, cupboards, even the clothes in my wardrobe had all been rifled. Now I knew why.

After a long, fruitless search of my own, I slumped down despondently into an armchair and took out my pipe. Plunging my hand into the tobacco jar at my elbow, I felt something curious. I could hardly believe it. There in my grasp was the very thing I'd been hunting for.

I flipped through the pages of the little black book, hoping to find some answers, but the whole thing was written in code.

While I consider myself as being pretty sharp when it comes to cyphers, after an hour or so racking my brain I was no further forward. I realized this puzzle would take time to crack.

My only hope was to lie low somewhere remote until I had the evidence to make the Government take Scudder's warning seriously. The Scottish Borders seemed the best bet.

I edged slowly to the window and looked down at the street. It was empty, save for a tall figure standing on the corner opposite. Was he a member of the Black Stone? Had he seen me return? I couldn't take any chances.

Quickly, I changed out of my evening clothes and into a sturdy tweed suit. Glancing at the railway timetable, I stuffed Scudder's notebook and a few essentials into my pockets. The fire escape outside the kitchen led me down to a deserted alleyway at the rear of the building. So far, so good.

I checked my watch and broke into a sprint. The express train to Scotland would be leaving Saint Pancras in ten minutes.

Chapter 3

On the run

When I reached the station there was no time to buy a ticket. I barged past the platform officials, and jumped into the last carriage of the Scottish express with seconds to spare.

As the train rattled north, I pulled Scudder's notebook from my pocket. I was pretty certain that all I needed was a keyword to unlock the code. But as the hours passed, everything I tried failed to make any sense.

Eventually I dozed off, and I only just woke in time to change at Dumfries. A slow Galloway train took me through a land of little wooded glens to a great wide moorland, gleaming with lochs and fringed by hills.

As the compartment filled with locals, I felt as if every one of them was eyeing me with suspicion.

Then I caught sight of something that only heightened my anxiety. The man next to me had a copy of the mid-day edition of *The Scotsman*. There on the front page screamed a headline that made my blood run cold.

PORTLAND PLACE MURDER

Killer flees north?

POLICE investigating the brutal murder of an as yet un-

The police would have wasted no time contacting the ports and stations with my description. Those officials at Saint Pancras must have remembered me.

I suddenly became aware of two men opposite who were engrossed in the same newspaper. They must have read the report. Was there a description of me? Had I already been recognized? I felt as if half a dozen pairs of eyes were boring into my very soul.

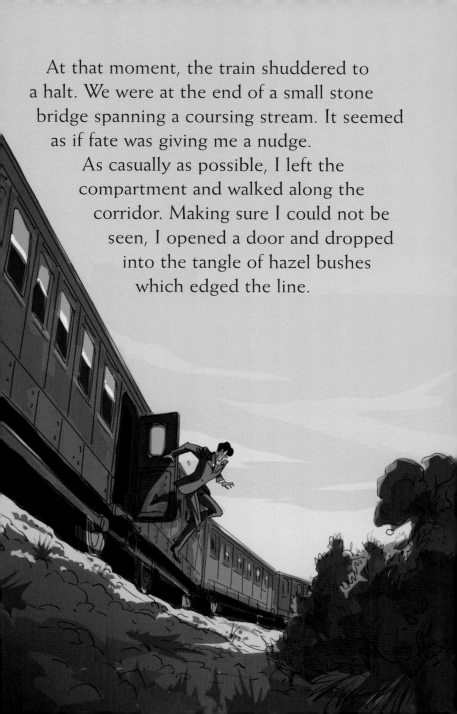

At that moment, the train shuddered to a halt. We were at the end of a small stone bridge spanning a coursing stream. It seemed as if fate was giving me a nudge.

As casually as possible, I left the compartment and walked along the corridor. Making sure I could not be seen, I opened a door and dropped into the tangle of hazel bushes which edged the line.

I scrambled through the thicket, reached the edge of the stream and soon found cover in the bushes a hundred yards away.

From my hiding place, I could see the reason for the train's sudden halt. A stray sheep had wandered onto the line ahead. Luckily, the guard who had already alighted to remove this obstruction had clearly been too busy to notice me. He herded the beast clear of the track, and within five minutes the train was on its way.

I only hoped that no one on board had witnessed my dramatic departure.

Chapter 4

Code breaker

There was no time to dwell on what might have been a hasty decision. I broke cover and continued my journey across country.

At about six that evening, I came to a rough stretch of road where the welcoming lights of a solitary inn sparkled in the twilight.

A good night's rest did wonders for my optimism, and the next morning I felt ready to pit myself against Scudder's code once more.

For the best part of three hours I wrestled with the contents of the little black book, until finally it dawned on me. What if 'Black Stone' were the keywords?

A few minutes' frantic scribbling proved me right, and soon I had the bones of Scudder's discoveries in front of me.

They didn't make for pleasant reading. Scudder believed that immediately after Karolides' death, top secret details of British military security were to be stolen from a diplomat who was due to convey them to our allies in France. The thieves would hand this information to the German Government. Being thus assured of victory, Germany would declare war on Britain.

Despite my efforts, the precise meaning of some of Scudder's notes remained obscure, such as a dozen odd references to *thirty-nine steps*. Their last mention was followed by the phrase *I counted them – 10:17 p.m., high tide*. I could only hope they weren't important.

Whatever the significance of these cryptic passages, the basic knowledge I had in my possession was explosive enough to be taken seriously. Somehow I had to alert the authorities.

At that moment, I heard the sound of a motor car approaching. I went to the window and saw a big touring car pull up a few hundred yards away. Two men got out and walked towards the inn. One was squat and muscular. The other bore a worrying resemblance to the tall man who had witnessed my departure from Portland Place.

I crept along the corridor to the hallway. From there I could hear what was said in the lobby without being seen.

Momentarily I heard the front door open and the two men enter. They were greeted by the innkeeper to whom they proceeded to give an all too accurate description of myself.

I didn't wait to hear any more. I scuttled back to my room, opened the window and scrambled outside. Keeping low, I ran past the inn and along the road to the men's car. I started it and, sending up a shower of gravel, raced away from the inn as fast as I could.

Chapter 5

Attack from above

Any doubts I might have had as to whether the Black Stone were on to me vanished in an instant.

I drove the forty horse-power tourer across the moor roads for all she was worth. I could only hope that having deprived my enemies of their vehicle, I could put a fair distance between them and myself.

After half an hour or so, I dared to hope that I'd shaken off my pursuers. Then, glancing behind me, I saw something that set my pulse racing. Far in the distance, a monoplane flew low over the hilltops. For a moment this sinister craft circled as if getting its bearings. Then, with a burst of speed, it headed straight in my direction.

If my stalkers had taken to the air, then my chances of evading them were dramatically reduced. On the bare moor I was at their mercy. My only chance was to get to the leafy cover of the valley.

I hurtled down the hillside like lightning. The bumpy roads were better designed for sheep than motor cars, and it felt as if my bones might rattle clean through my skin.

I had no choice but to go on, looking back whenever I dared, only to see the plane getting closer and closer.

Soon I was on a road between hedges. The noise of the aircraft seemed fainter behind me now, and I let my concentration slip for a second.

At that moment, I caught sight of the nose of another vehicle emerging at ninety degrees from a driveway ahead of me.

The road was too narrow to steer around the other car, so I did the only thing possible. I crashed into the hedge on the other side of the road.

As hawthorn branches scratched at my face, I sensed the ground beneath the car give way. To my horror, I realized that the hedge bordered a sheer drop to a river, some thirty feet or more below.

I felt the car buck and pitch. Then something hit me full on the head. I had a vague sense of an almighty smash, then nothing.

Chapter 6

Manhunt

"Steady there, old chap," came a warm, friendly voice.

As I blinked back into consciousness, the figure of a tall young man in tweeds formed before me.

He pressed a glass into my hand and I gulped down the contents gratefully.

I found myself lying on a sofa in what seemed to be some grand manor house.

"I must apologize for pulling out in front of you like that," he said. "Bad show."

"Er, no, it was my fault," I rambled. "You're not hurt, Mr....?"

"Bullivant, Sir Harry Bullivant. No, not a scratch, dear boy. Which is more than can be said for your motor car, I'm afraid."

"It seems I have you to thank for my lucky

escape," I said, rubbing my sore head.

"Thank that hawthorn branch, old man," he said with a chuckle. "Hooked you like a jolly old salmon and left you dangling. I just reeled you in, so to speak."

Over dinner, I engaged in the most pleasant conversation with my new friend, without giving away too much about myself.

It emerged that Sir Harry was the Liberal candidate for the nearby town of Brattleburn.

As we finished dinner he told me that politics ran in his family, as his uncle was the Permanent Secretary at the Foreign Office.

This news forced me to reconsider my secrecy. Here was someone with a link to the authorities. Today was the thirteenth. If Scudder was right, the attempt on Karolides' life would be made the day after tomorrow. I had to take a chance.

"Listen here, old man," I said. "I've something of a confession to make." I proceeded to tell him the whole story. He listened patiently, and when I'd finished he sat thoughtfully for a minute.

"I may be a bit of a chump as a politician, but I can size a chap up," he said at last. "You're no murderer, and I believe you're speaking the truth. Now, what can I do to help?"

We arranged a plan. He would telephone his uncle, Sir Walter, telling him to expect me at his country home in Wiltshire where I would deliver Scudder's information in person.

Harry offered me the use of his car, but I decided I would be less conspicuous journeying on foot, cross-country.

After a night's rest, a change of clothes and a hearty breakfast, I took my leave of my new ally and headed south towards the nearest railway station at Moffat.

But I had only been walking for half an hour when I became aware that I was not the only soul in the tangle of glens that morning. Just over a ridge, in the far distance, I could make out the heads of a string of men — it was the police, assisted by shepherds or gamekeepers by the looks of them.

They hallooed at the sight of me, and I could tell by their sudden excitement that Richard Hannay was their quarry, rather than some unfortunate fowl.

I ran for what felt like several miles.
Breathlessly I breasted the top of a ridge
and suddenly found myself in the grounds of
a whitewashed house. My pursuers had left
me no room to retreat. I had no choice. I'd
have to take my chances inside the building. I
sprinted across the lawn and walked through
a pair of French windows into a small study.
There, seated at a desk, was an elderly, bald
headed gentleman. He didn't move, but
simply stared at me with raised eyebrows.

"You seem in a hurry, my friend," he said calmly. Unable to catch my breath, I nodded towards the window at the line of approaching men.

"A fugitive from justice, eh?" he said. "Well, we can discuss it at length later. In the meantime, I've no desire to have clumsy rural policemen disturbing my peace." With that, he ushered me down a hallway and into a tiny cupboard-like room. "You will be safe enough here," he said, before closing the door behind him with a click.

Hardly able to believe my luck at the gentleman's kindness, I crouched in the darkness. As the minutes passed, I could make out neither the sound of my protector nor my pursuers. Then suddenly the door opened and the old man reappeared.

"They've gone," he assured me. But my relief was cut short by his very next words. "This is a lucky morning for you, Mr. Richard Hannay."

Before I had time to take this in, the old man raised a revolver to my head.

A glance at the man's right hand confirmed what I should have realized the moment I set foot in the house.

I was face to face with the leader of the Black Stone.

Chapter 7

The lair of the Black Stone

"Let us not waste time with formalities," said my captor, extending that tell-tale hand. "The notebook if you please."

"What notebook?" I replied flatly.

"Come now, Mr. Hannay," he said with a cruel smile, "We've both come too far to play games." As if to emphasize this point, he inched his revolver closer to my head.

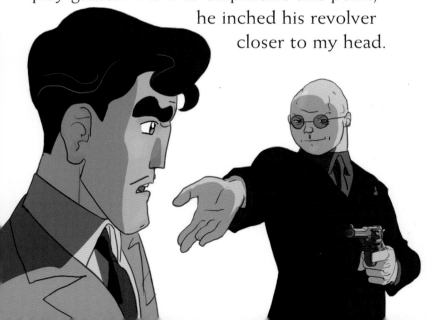

"Who is this Hannay, guv'nor?" I said, trying to sound more confident than I felt. "Ned Ainslie's my name, and so help me I wish I'd never gone and pinched that cursed motor car."

For a second I saw the villain's eyes flicker with doubt. He gestured with the gun for me to leave the room. Keeping me covered all the while, he frog-marched me back into the study. Then he rang a small bell and two men entered. I recognized them at once as the sinister characters from the inn.

"Well, Franz?" asked the bald man.

"That's him," said the taller of the new arrivals.

"Relieve Mr. Hannay of the contents of his pockets, Karl," ordered his boss.

The squat fellow grabbed me roughly and disgorged what little I had onto the table. To my surprise, I realized that the notebook was missing.

The bald man's voice took on an impatient tone. "Where is it?" he rasped threateningly.

"I already told you, guv'nor..." I began.

"Lock him up!" barked the chief to his lackeys. "We'll see if a spell without food and water loosens his tongue."

I found myself being manhandled across a courtyard and into a damp, pitch black storeroom attached to the main house. As my jailers turned the key in the lock, I tried to make out anything that might aid my escape.

After groping around various crates and sacks of grain, I found a cupboard. It was locked, but I managed to force it open. On the shelf in front of me were a box of matches and several electric lamps. Taking one, I examined the rest of the contents.

There was a carton of detonators, cord for fuses, and a dozen little bricks. Crumbling one in my hand, I recognized it at once as lentonite. I hadn't been a mining engineer for nothing. With just one of these bricks I could blow the house to smithereens.

I picked up a detonator and attached it to a couple of feet of fuse. Then I put the detonator in a quarter of a lentonite brick and buried it under a sack near the door.

Crouching as far away as possible, I lit the fuse and waited. I only hoped that I would survive the next few moments intact.

Suddenly a wave of heat surged from the floor. Then the wall opposite flashed a golden yellow and dissolved with a thunderous roar that hammered my brain into a pulp.

At first, I felt myself being choked by thick yellow fumes. But then fresh air wafted in from a ragged rent in the wall.

Clambering over the debris, I stepped through the hole and out into the yard.

I could hear confused cries coming from the house. Running blindly through the smoke, I managed to find my way to the fringe of trees that surrounded the building.

Then I kept running until I had put a good two miles between myself and the villains' lair.

Chapter 8

Assassination

After an hour or so tramping across country, I finally reached the town of Moffat. As I approached the station, my heart was lifted by the sight of young Harry Bullivant.

"Thank heavens," he cried. "I thought I might have missed you. I say, you do look a fright."

I swiftly related my encounter with the Black Stone.

He responded by putting his hand into his pocket and producing a familiar black tome.

"Scudder's notebook!" I gasped.

"I had you down as a chump for leaving it in your old jacket pocket, dear boy. But I reckon that little blunder saved your skin."

I thanked my new friend profusely and after he had lent me the rail fare to Wiltshire, I bade him a sad farewell.

Harry's uncle turned out to be a square-jawed fellow who welcomed me into his home as if I were family. I showed him Scudder's notebook and told him of the young man's warning regarding Karolides. It emerged that Scudder had been known to the British Secret Service and was highly regarded.

Sir Walter was persuaded some dark business was imminent, but to my surprise he dismissed Scudder's theory about an assassination as fanciful. "In any case," he added, "Karolides is too well guarded."

After a bath, a shave and a change of clothes, I explained everything that had occurred to me, from the death of Scudder to my encounter with the Black Stone.

"Being chased right into the very house they'd rented was a stroke of bad luck," said Sir Walter.

"I still don't know how the local police got onto me," I said.

"After Harry telephoned, I did a bit of research on your adventures," said Sir Walter. "It seems the innkeeper told the police about the car you stole. They found the wreckage and then picked up your trail nearby."

"I suppose I'm still a wanted man," I said with a sigh.

"Oh, I've sorted all that out with Scotland Yard, dear boy," said Sir Walter, with a reassuring smile.

We spent the next few hours poring over Scudder's notes, interrupted only when Sir Walter had to leave the room to take a telephone call.

When the distinguished man returned, his face was ashen.

"It seems I owe our late friend Scudder an apology," he said sadly. "Karolides has been shot dead."

Chapter 9

The imposter

I glanced at my watch. It was a few minutes after midnight. Karolides had been murdered on the fifteenth just as Scudder had predicted.

"War is inevitable now," said Sir Walter. "We shall have to bring Royer's visit forward."

"Royer?"

"The French diplomat. He'll be taking the details of Britain's military security to France."

"Can't you cancel it?" I asked.

"No, we must carry on as planned," replied Sir Walter. "It's vital to the safety of Britain and her allies in the times that lie ahead."

After a few hours' sleep, Sir Walter and I drove to his house in London. It was here that the meeting with Royer was to take place.

That evening, I watched nervously from the balcony overlooking the hall as Royer and a stream of well-known officials arrived at the house and walked past into the meeting room.

I remained at my post for over an hour. Then, at half past ten, the door of the room opened and the First Sea Lord came out. At least that was my first thought. I had seen that familiar face in newspapers and magazines a hundred times – the trim beard, the firm fighting mouth and the blunt square nose. Yet, at that moment, as he glanced up and caught my gaze, I spotted a look of recognition in his keen blue eyes, even though we had never met.

As he made a hasty exit, I rushed down the staircase and picked up the telephone. A few seconds later I was connected with the Sea Lord's residence.

"Is his Lordship at home?" I asked.

"His Lordship retired to bed an hour ago," said the servant. "He is unwell tonight."

It seemed my part in this business was not yet ended. I marched into the meeting room and was met by the questioning faces of the assembled officials.

"Gentlemen," I announced, "the man who just left this room was an imposter."

Chapter 10

A race against time

"Impossible!" snorted Travers, the official from the Admiralty.

"Don't you see the cleverness of it?" I said. "You were too interested in other things to question whether or not the First Sea Lord had been invited. It was natural for him to be here, and that put you off your guard."

"The young man is right," said Royer. "His psychology is good. Our enemies have not been foolish."

"But the fiend heard everything," said Travers. "The security plans, not only of this country, but also those of France."

"Then we're done for," I said.

"No, my friend," said Royer. "I know something of the habits of the spy.

He delivers his intelligence in person and receives his reward in person."

I was filled with renewed enthusiasm. "Then if we can intercept the Black Stone before they can leave the country..."

"But we've no way of knowing where they'll leave from," said the War Minister.

Suddenly I had a flash of inspiration.

"The thirty-nine steps!" I cried.

The Minister looked at me as if I had gone mad.

"There was a phrase in Scudder's notebook," I explained, *"Thirty-nine steps — I counted them — 10:17 p.m., high tide."*

"Then we've less than twenty-four hours to find them," said Sir Walter.

"Right, gentlemen," I said purposefully. "We'll need a book of Tide Tables."

Minutes later, we were at the Admiralty, scanning the locations where high tide occurred at 10:17.

At first it looked a hopeless task. That time covered at least fifty places.

We had to narrow it down.

Where would a man in a hurry leave for Germany? Somewhere on the Southeast coast I reasoned. That would provide the quickest crossing to Ostend or Antwerp.

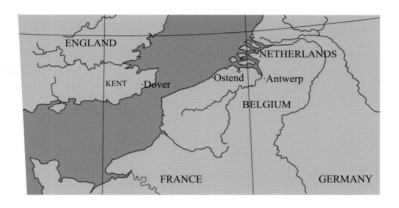

There were no regular night steamers at 10:17, so they must plan to use a private yacht or boat that would require a high tide to launch from shore.

Then there were the steps. It didn't sound like a dock somehow. It must be some place where there were several staircases, with one marked out from the others by having thirty-nine steps.

The Inspector of Coastguards was called for, and after a process of elimination we finally came up with a location – the Ruff.

"It's a big chalk headland in Kent," explained the coastguard man. "It has lots of villas on the top, and some of them have staircases down to a private beach."

I looked around the assembled company. "If one of those staircases has thirty-nine steps gentlemen, then we've solved the mystery."

Chapter 11

The thirty-nine steps

By ten o'clock the next morning, I found myself on a clifftop overlooking a row of quaint villas on the Kent coast.

I was joined by Scaife, an Inspector from Scotland Yard with naval experience. He had just returned from a closer study of the staircases of each house.

"There's only one with thirty-nine steps," he announced.

I almost jumped up and cheered at the news.

"Place called Trafalgar Lodge," he went on. "Belongs to a respectable old gent called Appleton, according to the house-agent."

At that moment a yacht came into the bay. She looked about a hundred and fifty tons and was flying a white ensign that marked her as one of our own.

"Might be innocent enough," said Scaife. "I'll go and investigate."

So it was that, thirty minutes later, I watched as a small fishing boat made its way to within a few feet of the yacht.

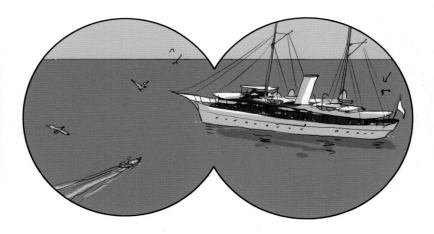

I saw Scaife, looking every inch the local angler, call up to the larger craft. Some uniformed crew members appeared on the deck of the yacht and a brief conversation followed. Then Scaife departed and was back at my side within an hour.

"She's called the Ariadne," he said. "The officers and crew sound as English as you or I, but..."

"What?" I asked anxiously.

Scaife looked thoughtful. "There was nothing English about the captain's close-cropped hair or the cut of his collar and tie."

"That settles it," I declared. "It's time I paid a visit to Trafalgar Lodge."

It was just after nine o'clock that I made my way up the path of that humble little villa. A search warrant from Scaife nestled in my breast pocket, next to my racing heart.

The door was answered by a young maid. I told her my name was Smith. After leaving me alone in the hall for a moment, she returned.

I was ushered into a large drawing room overlooking the garden, with the sea beyond.

But it wasn't the view that first caught my eye as I entered the room. It was the three figures in evening dress standing before me.

Their features may have been subtly altered by the use of false hair pieces, but I was convinced that these men were the trio who had held me captive in Scotland.

The maid introduced me and withdrew. "Mr. Smith?" said the white-haired old man claiming to be Appleton. "I don't believe I've made your acquaintance."

"Save your breath, sir," I said, with all the courage I could muster. "The game's up. I have here a warrant for the arrest of you three gentlemen."

The old man looked shocked.

"Arrest?" he said. "Good grief, what for?"

"For the murder of Franklin P. Scudder on the 11th of June," I replied.

The tall man raised an eyebrow. "Oh, the Portland Place business. I read about it. But you're quite mistaken," he said nonchalantly, "I, for one, was in a nursing home at the time."

"I was out of the country," said the stocky fellow, adjusting his tie in the mirror.

"And I dined at my club until late that night," added the old man, stroking his white beard.

For a split second I wondered if I'd made the most terrible blunder.

"So you see you are mistaken, young man," said the old man respectfully. "Now if you don't mind," he added, "we are late for an engagement."

I decided to take a chance. "I'm most terribly sorry, sir," I said, removing my leather glove and extending my right hand. "No hard feelings?"

Instinctively, the old gentleman removed his white evening glove to shake hands. In that instant, he realized his mistake. But it was too late. Both our eyes rested on the fourth finger of his bare right hand.

Suddenly, he kicked over a table and produced a revolver from his pocket.

"Schnell, Franz," he cried, "das Boot, das Boot!" The tall man and his compatriot made a dash for the door, but ran straight into Scaife's men who were stationed outside. The old man fired a shot at the police and Franz managed to struggle free. I lunged at the old man and tackled him to the ground, sending his weapon flying from his hand. I dragged him to his feet, just in time to see Franz descend the steps to the waiting yacht.

"He is safe," cried the old man. "You cannot follow in time. Der Schwarzestein has triumphed."

"Not for long, my fine friend," I said, as I clinked a pair of handcuffs around my prisoner's wrists. "You see, for the last hour, the Ariadne has been in British hands. Those steps lead straight to the hangman's noose."

As you will know, Sir Walter was proved right. War was declared a few weeks later, and I joined up immediately to fight for King and country.

But I still think I'd done my best service before I even put on my uniform.

John Buchan 1875-1940

John Buchan was born in
Perth, Scotland and began his
writing career while studying at
Glasgow University.

After graduating, he worked
at the British High Commission
in South Africa, a country
which would later feature in many of his books.

On his return to Britain he trained as a lawyer,
but when the First World War broke out in 1914
he became a newspaper reporter in France.

He was elected as a Scottish Unionist Member
of Parliament in 1927 and was later made
Governor-General of Canada in 1935.

He wrote over thirty thriller novels, including
five books about the adventures of Richard
Hannay. *The Thirty-Nine Steps* (1915) was the first,
and it remains his most famous work. It has gone
on to be adapted many times for the stage, film
and television.

Series editor: Lesley Sims

First published in 2010 by Usborne Publishing Ltd., Usborne House, 83-85 Saffron
Hill, London EC1N 8RT, England. www.usborne.com Copyright © 2010 Usborne
Publishing Ltd. All rights reserved. No part of this publication may be reproduced,
stored in a retrieval system or transmitted in any form or by any means, electronic,
mechanical, photocopying, recording or otherwise, without the prior permission of
the publisher. The name Usborne and the devices ♀ ⊕ are Trade Marks of Usborne
Publishing Ltd. UE. First published in America in 2011.